Dilly
and the
Birthday Treat

Tony Bradman

Illustrated by
Susan Hellard

For Lily, Oscar and Joe
T.B.

EGMONT
We bring stories to life

Book Band: Purple

First published in Great Britain 2011
by Egmont UK Ltd
239 Kensington High Street, London W8 6SA
Text copyright © Tony Bradman 2011
Illustrations copyright © Susan Hellard 2011
The author and illustrator have asserted their moral rights.
ISBN 978 1 14052 5303 1
10 9 8 7 6 5 4 3 2 1
A CIP catalogue record for this title is available from the British Library.
Printed in Singapore.

Dilly

and the
Birthday Treat

Blue Bananas

Father was having a bad day, and it wasn't even lunchtime yet.

'For heaven's sake, Dilly!' he yelled.

'Do you have to be so noisy? I can hardly hear what your sister is saying!'

'Duh! Of course I do, Father,' said Dilly.
'I'm playing a noisy game. Dorla is
probably being boring, anyway.'

'Actually, I was asking Father what he wanted for his birthday,' said Dorla. 'I'm going to get him something special.'

'So am I!' said Dilly. Then he frowned.

'Er . . . what would you like, Father?'

'I'd like you to be well behaved for just one day, Dilly,' Father said with a sigh. 'Now that really would be a treat.'

'Huh, you'll be lucky,' muttered Dorla.
'You shut up, stinky old Dorla!' Dilly
snapped. 'I could do it if I wanted to.'
Dorla stuck her tongue out at Dilly,
and he did the same back to her.

9

'That will do, you two,' said Father.
'Actually, Dilly, I'll be happy if you
behave yourself for the next half hour.
But I won't hold my breath.'

Dilly scowled, and opened his mouth
as if he had something else to say . . .
But then he seemed to change his
mind, and stomped off.

11

And of course, within five minutes he was misbehaving again . . .

CRASH! BANG! TINKLE . . .

A week later it was Father's birthday.
Dorla got up early and ran into
Mother and Father's bedroom. Dilly
followed her in, and stood at the end
of their bed.

Dorla gave Father the card and present she had made.

Gosh!

'A bookmark!' said Father. 'Why, thank you, Dorla, it's lovely.'

14

Mother gave Father a nice card too,

and some terrific presents.

'Your turn, Dilly,' said Mother.
'I know he's got something for you,
dear, although he wouldn't tell me
what it is. It's all a bit of a mystery.'

'That sounds interesting!' said Father.
'Well, Dilly, hand it over.'

Dilly gave Father a small envelope.
Inside it was a card Dilly had
made . . . and nothing else. Father
was rather puzzled, and read out
what Dilly had written.

Happy birthday, Father!

I promise to be well behaved

for the whole day!

Lots of love, Dilly xxx

'Oh, I see!' said Father, and laughed.

'That's very funny, Dilly.'

'This isn't a joke, Father,' said Dilly, frowning. 'I'm serious.'

'Really?' said Father, surprised. 'Well, it's a nice idea, but I'll be amazed if you can manage it. Now, I think it's time we had breakfast . . .'

Usually breakfast was a disaster with Dilly. But today he was very well behaved. He didn't make disgusting noises or even throw food at Dorla.

And when he had finished he
asked nicely if he could get down
from the table.

'Of course you can,' said Father. 'And er . . . well done for being so good.'

'Yes, that was the most peaceful breakfast we've had since before you were born, Dilly,' said Mother.

'You've certainly made a great start to the day.'

'There's a long way to go,' muttered
Dorla. 'Hours and hours, in fact.'
'No problem,' said Dilly with a sniff,
and left the kitchen.

Father and Mother looked at each
other for a moment – then they shook
their heads and sighed. They were sure
Dilly would soon be back to normal.

After breakfast, Mother went to work.
But Father was having the day off.
'Come on, you two,' he said once he
had tidied up. 'Let's go to the park.'

Dorla and Dilly went into the
playground and had lots of fun.

Although one little
dinosaur kept
pushing Dilly, and
tried to trip him up
a couple of times . . .

Father didn't see what was going on
until it was too late. Dilly was scowling
at the little dinosaur, and his tail was
quivering like it does just before he
loses his temper and lets loose with a
150-mile-per-hour super-scream . . .

'Here we go,' said Dorla, a grin on her face and her paws over her ears.

Father held his breath, waiting for the
inevitable to happen. But it didn't.
Dilly simply turned on his heel and
walked away. And he was smiling.

'I don't believe it,' Father murmured.
Dorla was pretty shocked as well.

There were more shocks to come.

They had to go to the supermarket, and usually Dilly was very badly behaved there. It was full of shelves to climb, trolleys to be crashed into each other, tempting towers of tins to topple . . .

But Dilly didn't misbehave in the
supermarket at all. He was calm and
very helpful.

And that afternoon at home he played quiet games, and didn't argue with Dorla once –

even though she tried as hard as she could to upset him.

By the time Mother came home, Father couldn't stop himself grinning.

'I think we've made a real
breakthrough!' he said. 'You've been
such a good little dinosaur today,
Dilly! I was sure you couldn't do it.
I'm so impressed!'

'Oh, it was nothing,' Dilly said
modestly. 'Can we have the cake now?'

There were lots and lots of candles on
the birthday cake, and it was delicious.

They sang 'Happy Birthday' to Father,
and had a lovely evening playing games
and watching TV.

And then Dilly went to bed without complaining once.

40

The next morning at breakfast, Father

smiled at Dilly and gave him a kiss.

'Thanks for yesterday, Dilly,' he said.
'It was a fantastic birthday treat. I
wondered if you might be able to keep
up the good behaviour from now on . . .'

'Sure, why not?' said Dilly with a shrug, and Father beamed.

'Although . . . ' Dilly added, 'would it be OK if I was just a little bit naughty sometimes?'

'Oh, I should think so,' laughed Father.
'Nobody's perfect, after all.'

'Great!' yelled Dilly. He jumped down from the table and dashed off.

The smile faded from Father's face,
and he winced with every sound.
'Oh well,' he said with a sigh. 'There's
always my birthday next year . . .'

Oh dear. . .

But Dilly was too busy having fun to hear him.